Why Do Dogs Bark?

by JOAN HOLUB

illustrations by Anna DiVito

Dial Books for Young Readers
New York

Published by Dial Books for Young Readers
A division of Penguin Putnam Inc.
345 Hudson Street
New York, New York 10014

First published by Dial Books for Young Readers and Puffin Books,
divisions of Penguin Putnam Books for Young Readers, 2001

1 3 5 7 9 10 8 6 4 2

Printed in Hong Kong
Text set in ITC Century Book

The Dial Easy-to-Read logo is a registered trademark
of Dial Books for Young Readers,
a division of Penguin Putnam Inc., ®TM 1,162, 718.

LIBRARY OF CONGRESS CATALOGING-IN-PUBLICATION DATA
Holub, Joan.
Why do dogs bark? / by Joan Holub.
p. cm.
Summary: Questions and answers present information about the origins, behavior,
and characteristics of dogs and their interaction with humans.
ISBN 0-8037-2504-3 (hardcover)
1. Dogs—Behavior—Miscellanea—Juvenile literature. 2. Dogs—Miscellanea—Juvenile literature.
[1. Dogs—Miscellanea. 2. Questions and answers.] I. Title.
SF433.H68 2001 636.7—dc21 00-023984

Reading Level 2.4

Photo Credits

Front cover; pages 7, 9 (Australian Shepherd, Mixed Breed and Boston Terrier),
25, 33, 45 copyright © Davis/Lynn Images
Pages 1, 5 (Golden Retriever), 10, 11, 14 (two wolves–D.Robert Franz), 15 (Rita
Summers), 18, 21, 23, 36, 37, 38, 39, 48 copyright © Ron Kimball Studios
Pages 13, 34 copyright © Elizabeth Hathon

*With thanks to Joy and Dena,
my wonderful editors*

*Thanks to Stephen Zawistowski, PH.D.,
Certified Applied Animal Behaviorist, for his help*—J.H.

For Michael and Stephen Olinger—A.D.

Do you love dogs?

Many people love dogs.

Dogs are even called "man's best friend."

There are over one hundred kinds,

or breeds, of pet dogs.

Some popular breeds are retrievers,
cocker spaniels, poodles, beagles,
Rottweilers (ROT-wy-lerz),
and German shepherds.
Dogs that are a mix of breeds
are called mixed-breeds or mutts.

Which dogs are smallest and biggest?

Dogs come in many different shapes
and sizes.

Chihuahuas (chuh-WAH-waz) are
the smallest dogs.

A Teacup Chihuahua will fit in your hand.

Mastiffs and Saint Bernards are
the biggest dogs.

They can weigh over 250 pounds.

That is about as much as four kids
your age!

Which dogs are best?

No one breed of dog is best

at everything.

But many breeds have special skills.

Greyhounds can run very fast.

They have powerful legs and thin bodies.

Some can run forty miles an hour.

Terriers (TER-ee-urz) are brave.

They will hunt animals that are

much larger than they are.

Retrievers (ree-TREE-vurz) are

great swimmers.

They have webbed toes

to help them swim.

They can even swim underwater.

What can your dog do best?

How many puppies can a dog have at one time?

A group of puppies born at one time is called a litter.

A mother dog can have many puppies in one litter.

Five is the most common number.

One dog had a litter
of twenty-two puppies!
Newborn puppies of all breeds
look a lot alike.
It can be hard to tell what breed
a newborn puppy is.

How does a puppy grow up to be a dog?

Puppies are born with their eyes closed.
They can't see or hear until they are
two to three weeks old.

When puppies are three to four weeks
old, they begin to walk, bark, play,
and wag their tails.

Puppies drink milk from their mothers
until they are five to seven weeks old.
They may also lick their mother's face,
so she'll spit up food for them to eat.
Then they are usually ready
to eat puppy food.
Most puppies become full-grown dogs
when they are one year old.

Are dogs related to wolves?

Yes! A long time ago, there were no dogs.

Then people taught some wolves

to be helpful.

Over hundreds of years, some of these

wolves changed.

They became the dogs we have today.

Other wolves did not change.

They are still wild.

What is a pack of dogs or wolves?

A pack is like a dog's family.

Dogs and wolves like to eat, play,

and sleep with their pack.

Each pack has one leader.

Your dog thinks your family is its pack.

It thinks someone in your family

is the leader.

Do you know who?

Why do dogs bark?

Your dog barks to protect your house
and yard.
When a stranger comes around,
it barks to sound an alarm.
It wants to tell you and your family
that a stranger is nearby.

Your dog may also bark to tell a stranger to go away.

Some dogs bark to greet their owners when they come home.

Why do dogs howl?

Some dogs howl when they are lonely.
If your dog is alone for too long,
it may howl.
It is trying to find you or
its dog friends.
Other dogs may howl
back to say hello.

Some dogs howl when they hear singing,
music, or sirens.

They think it sounds like other dogs
howling, so they want to howl back.

Why do dogs bury bones?

Dogs and wolves almost always

want to eat.

Wolves must work hard to find food.

They eat fast, before other animals

can steal their food.

That is where the saying "wolf it down"

comes from.

When wolves have extra food,

they bury it to save it for later.

Pet dogs also worry that someone
will take their food.

So they eat fast too.

Some pet dogs bury or hide bones
to save them for later.

Does your dog do this?

Can dogs see better than people?

Dogs can see better than people can at night.

They are also better at seeing movement from far away.

But dogs do not see colors very well.

They can see the color blue.

But most other colors look gray to a dog.

Can dogs hear better than people?

Yes! Dogs can hear high tones and soft sounds that people can't hear. You can't hear the high sound of a dog whistle, but your dog can. Dogs can also tell which direction a sound is coming from better than you can.

Why do dogs sniff you?

Smell is a dog's most important sense.

A dog's sense of smell is over one

hundred times better than your

sense of smell.

A dog sniffs you to find out who you are.

It can probably tell if you are afraid

by how you smell too.

Does your dog sniff you?

Your dog remembers how you smell

better than it remembers what you

look like.

Why do dogs lick people?

Dogs smell through their noses.

They also smell through

very tiny openings in their mouths

behind their top front teeth.

Licking can help dogs find out

who people and other dogs are.

Dogs may also lick people because

they like the taste of their salty skin.

Why do dogs pee so often on a walk?

Dogs pee to leave their own special smell behind.

They want other dogs to know they were there.

They are also saying, "This place is mine!"

Why do dogs roll in stinky stuff?

Dogs sometimes like to roll

in other animals' poop or in garbage.

They do this to cover their own smell.

In the wild, some animals run away

if they smell a dog or wolf nearby.

Dogs and wolves cover their smell

so they can sneak up on other animals.

Why do dogs pant?

When a dog pants, it breathes hard

and fast through its open mouth.

Dogs pant when they are too hot.

It helps them cool off.

People sweat to cool off.

But dogs cannot sweat through their fur.

They lose heat through their

tongues instead.

Why do dogs have bad breath?

Over time, slime forms on a dog's

teeth and gums.

This can smell bad.

Dogs can't brush their teeth.

Wouldn't you have bad breath

if you never brushed?

Why do dogs wag their tails?

Dogs wag their tails when they

are happy.

If a dog's tail is down between its

back legs, it is scared or unhappy.

When two dogs meet, their tails show

what they are thinking.

If their tails stick out straight,

they are deciding who is in charge.

If one dog's tail is high and the other's

is low, the high-tail dog is the boss.

What other ways do dogs talk with their bodies?

Your dog uses its body to show how it
feels and to tell you what it wants.
When your dog rolls onto its back,
it may be saying "You are the boss"
or "Rub my tummy."
If its tail and ears stand straight up and
it shows its teeth, your dog is angry.

When your dog holds out one paw,
it is asking you for something.
If your dog bows down on its front legs,
that usually means it wants to play.

What kinds of jobs can dogs do?

Your dog's job is to be your friend.

But dogs can do many other jobs.

Some bloodhounds help find lost people.

Their keen sense of smell also helps

them track criminals.

Sheepdogs and collies can herd.
They are good at rounding up sheep
or cows.

Some huskies pull snowsleds.
They have thick, warm fur
and lots of energy.

Some German shepherds are trained
to be Seeing Eye dogs or police dogs.
They are fast learners, very smart,
and good at obeying directions.

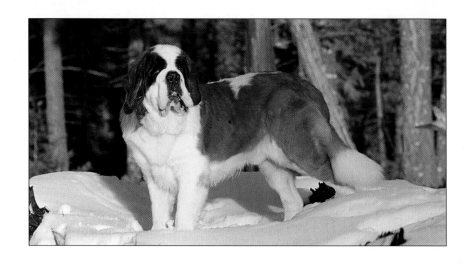

What other kinds of jobs can dogs do?

Saint Bernards are good at finding

people lost in snowstorms.

They have a very strong sense of smell.

They can also sense the body heat of

a person buried under snow.

Doberman Pinschers (DO-ber-mun PIN-

sherz) can be guard dogs.

They will bark to scare away strangers.

Some dogs are actors.

They are good at following directions

and staying calm.

They do not get upset by

the lights and noise on

a television or movie set.

Are any dogs heroes?

Balto

Many dogs have done brave things.

A sled dog named Balto once helped

carry medicine to a town in Alaska.

He ran for twenty hours in a snowstorm.

Without his help, many people

would have died.

Barry

A Saint Bernard named Barry

rescued many people

lost in snowstorms.

He once saved a small girl

who was buried in the snow.

He lay down next to her

to keep her warm.

Then he pulled her to a nearby house.

Buddy

A German shepherd named Buddy

was the first Seeing Eye dog.

Buddy was trained to help a blind man.

Buddy helped him cross streets safely.

For the first time, the man could

travel and go to work on his own,

thanks to Buddy.

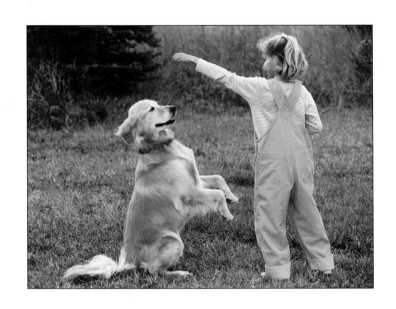

Do dogs understand words?

Experts think some dogs can learn

twenty or more words.

This helps make dogs easier

to train than many other animals.

Most dogs can learn the command words

sit, stay, and *come.*

Dogs may understand many other words.

How many words does your dog know?

good dog~

Training

When your dog is old enough,

you can teach it to obey and do tricks.

Train your dog for only

one to five minutes each time.

Teach one trick at a time.

Speak slowly and clearly.

Never hit or shout at your dog.

Always say "good dog" and give your dog

a treat, a hug, or a pat when it obeys.

Training your dog to sit

Hold a small treat over your dog's nose.
Move the treat backward
over your dog's head.
Gently push your dog's rear down
until it sits.
Each time your dog sits down,
say "sit," and give it the treat.

Training your dog to come

Stand about five steps away

from your dog.

Look into its eyes for a moment.

Then say "come."

Use hand movements, too.

Try to teach your dog to sit instead of

jumping up when it comes to you.

come

Training your dog to stay

Hold one hand out with your palm
facing your dog.

Say "stay."

Keep your hand out.

Step away from your dog slowly
and say "stay" over and over.

If your dog does not stay put, start again.

Most pet dogs want to be

their owner's best buddy.

Your dog loves you.

Take good care of your dog . . .

and it will be your friend forever.